Cecily G. and the 9 monkeys

By
H. A. REY

Houghton Mifflin Company · Boston

Here are the names of the nine monkeys in this book:

Mother Pamplemoose and Baby Jinny

Curious George who was clever, too

James who was good

Johnny who was brave

Arthur who was kind

David who was strong

and Punch and Judy, the twins

Library of Congress Cataloging-in-Publication Data

Rey, H. A. (Hans Augusto), date.
  Cecily G. and the 9 monkeys/by H. A. Rey.
    p. cm.
  Summary: A lonely giraffe teams up with the nine playful monkeys.
  ISBN 0-395-50651-4
  [1. Giraffes—Fiction. 2. Monkeys—Fiction.] I. Title.
II. Title: Cecily G. and the nine monkeys.
PZ7.R33Ce 1989   88-37188
[E]—dc19   CIP
                        AC

Printed in the United States of America

HOR RNF ISBN 0-395-18430-4
HOR PAP ISBN 0-395-50651-4

Twenty-Fourth Printing

This is Cecily G. Her whole name is Cecily Giraffe, but she is called Cecily G. or just plain Cecily for short.

One day she was very sad because all her family and all her friends had been taken away to a zoo. Cecily G. was all alone. She began to cry because she wanted someone to play with.

Now, in another place,
lived a mother monkey called
Mother Pamplemoose and eight little monkeys. They
were sad, too, because some woodcutters had cut down
all the trees in their forest, and monkeys have to have
trees to live in. One of the little monkeys was called
Curious George. He was a clever monkey. He said,
"We must pack up at once and go on a journey to find
a new home."

So they did. They walked and they walked and they
walked until they came to the bank of a deep river. They
couldn't get across and there wasn't any way around.
They didn't know *what* to do.

4

Suddenly Jinny, the baby monkey, pointed across to the other bank.

There stood Cecily Giraffe! When she saw the monkeys, she stopped crying. "Do you want to get across?" she said.

"Yes, yes!" they cried.

"Step back then," called Cecily G.

Yoop! With one big jump Cecily's front feet landed on the monkeys' side of the bank. And then she stood still.

Curious George was the first to see that Cecily had made herself into a bridge. He ran across. Then came Johnny, who was a brave monkey. Then all the others, one by one.

"Thank you, dear Giraffe," shouted George, "and please put your head down a little so that we can talk to you without shouting. That's better! What is your name and why are you sad?"

"My name is Cecily Giraffe, and I am unhappy because I haven't anyone to play with. Why are *you* sad?"

"We are sad," said George, "because we haven't anywhere to live."

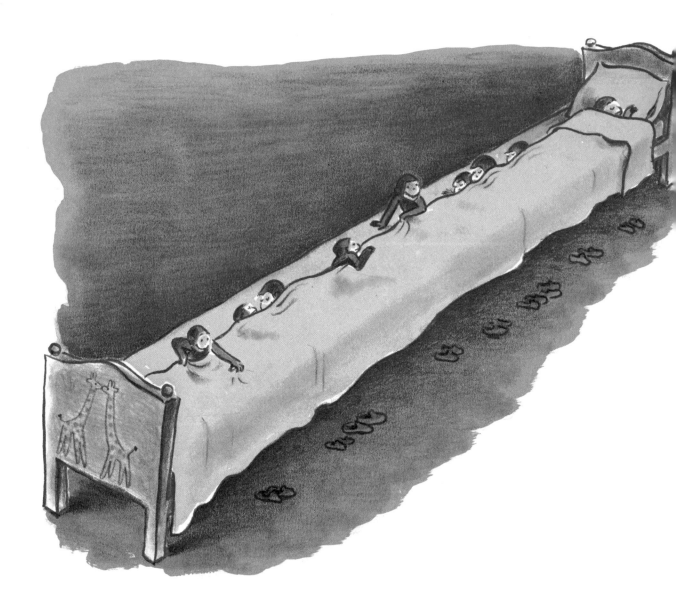

"Then why don't you stay with me for a while?" said Cecily. "My house is empty now."

"We'd love to," cried all the monkeys at once.

"Good!" said Cecily, and she smiled for the first time that day. "Now it is bedtime. I'll show you your room, and tomorrow we'll have some lovely games." So she tucked all the nine monkeys into one giraffe bed, and in a few minutes they were fast asleep.

Next morning, after a good night's sleep and a big breakfast, Cecily G. said, "Now let's play see-saw! James, you sit on my back. (James was a very good monkey and usually had first turn.) George, you climb on my head, and you, Johnny, sit on my hind feet. That's the way!"

"Now," they cried, "off we go!" Cecily stood up on her front legs. Up-down, up-down, up-down, went the see-saw.

After a while Cecily stopped and took on another load. Everyone had a turn; but baby Jinny got so excited that Mother Pamplemoose was afraid she would fall off. She had to climb down and give her place to James, who got an extra ride. Jinny cried a little, but Arthur, who was very kind, dried her tears and told her that he had an idea for another game that she could play better.

So Arthur whispered something to all the other monkeys. They rushed into the house where they had left their belongings and in a minute they were back with their skis.

"But there isn't any snow for skis," said Cecily G.

"Please," said George, "be so kind as to stretch your neck so I can tie your head to the top of that palm tree over there."

"I'll be glad to," said Cecily, and she did.

Then all the monkeys put on their skis, climbed the tree, and slid down Cecily's back, over and over again. Brave Johnny even did stunts. When he jumped he seemed to be flying.

After a while Cecily's neck got tired, but she was having such a good time that she hardly noticed. "You are a wonderful skier, Johnny," she said.

Johnny was so pleased he tried a specially high jump and — bump — down he fell, flat on his nose.

Mother Pamplemoose ran to pick him up. "I think it is time to play something else," she said. "Let's find a game that Cecily can play too."

"Yes, yes," cried all the monkeys.

Johnny thought very hard because he was such a good
monkey that he wanted Cecily to be sure and have fun,
too. All at once he had a wonderful idea. "We'll make
some *stilts* for Cecily G.," he cried.

Johnny and David, who was a very strong
monkey, cut down two palm trees.
The twins, Punch and Judy,
did the sawing.

James hammered
the nails.

George watched and gave advice. When the stilts were done, he proudly carried them to Cecily G. and showed her how to use them.

Cecily Giraffe was terribly excited.

All the monkeys helped and — up — UP — UP — she went — right into the sky —

so high the page isn't big enough to show all of her.

It was very hot the next day and they all thought it would be just the thing to go to the seashore.

After a short walk, they came to the beach and Mother Pamplemoose thought it would be nice to have a swim before lunch. But Johnny had been thinking. He asked Cecily to put down her head so that he could whisper in her ear.

Can you guess what he said? He wanted Cecily to be a —

SAILBOAT! And so Cecily made herself into a sailboat. Johnny was Captain. He shouted orders and

pulled the ropes. "Not so hard, not so hard!" cried
Cecily. But she was too late —

over they went, into the water.

"Quick, quick, climb on my back," called Cecily Giraffe, when Johnny cried for help.

In a minute they were safe on the beach, but Cecily was so wet and cold, they decided to take off her skin and hang it in the sun to dry.

"It is quite complicated to be a giraffe," said Punch to Judy as they brought Cecily the clothespins.

Cecily Giraffe had hardly gotten her skin back on again when a big black cloud came up and hid the sun.

"Oh — oh — it's going to rain —" cried the monkeys.

Off they rushed, and back they came, one-two, one-two, carrying their umbrellas on their shoulders.

But the rain didn't start at once and James thought it would be fun to use the umbrellas for a new game. He called it "Parachute-jumping."

Each monkey, one at a time, climbed up on Cecily's head, opened his umbrella and jumped off.

Down they floated. It was such fun they did it hundreds of times.

22

All went well until, all of a sudden,
Curious George tipped his umbrella
sideways to see something and —
thump — down he fell. When
he looked at his broken
umbrella, he sat down on
the ground to cry. And,
just at that moment, the
rain started. Poor George!
Great splashing drops began
to fall all around him.

"Quick, quick, climb
up my neck, George,"
said Cecily.

George climbed up and up until he was in the sunshine again, high above the rain cloud.

All week long Cecily and her new friends had great fun. When Sunday came, Cecily was so happy she decided to give a concert to celebrate. The monkeys thought it a splendid idea. Arthur made up a nice song for them all to sing together and George promised to play on the harp.

At last they were ready and George was just starting
them off when someone cried —

"Fire! Fire! Cecily's house is burning!"

The concert stopped almost before it started, but no one knew what to do to put out the fire.

"If only we had a ladder, we could throw water on the flames," cried Mother Pamplemoose.

"I know what to do," said James. "There's a pump near the house, and a hose, and Cecily can be the ladder."

Punch and Judy worked the pump and ——

George climbed up to turn the hose on the fire. James
stood on Cecily's back to guide the hose up to George.

In a minute the fire was out and Cecily's house was saved.

Cecily looked at the wet little monkeys and said, "Dear new friends, I don't know how to thank you. . . . Would you like to stay with me always? It would make me very happy."

"Oh, Cecily G.," cried Mother Pamplemoose, baby Jinny, curious George, brave Johnny, good little James, kind Arthur, strong David, and the twins, Punch and Judy, all together, "We'll stay with you for ever and ever. . . . And now let's finish our concert."

So they took hold of hands, danced round in a ring

and sang Arthur's song as loud as they could sing.

Nine lit-tle monks were we home-less and

in di-is - may till Ce-ci - ly Gi-

raff' had us a - long t-o stay

so here in a ri-ing we'll all dance and si-ing

Cec'-ly Cec'-ly we will ne-ver go a-way.

E   Rey, H. A.
REY   Cecily G. and the 9
           monkeys

PERMA-BOUND®

DATE DUE			

$11.00

ANDERSON ELEM
LIBRARY